BELOW
THE GREEN

Titles in the Below the Green series

To order copies of these, please go to
getbook.at/UndergroundAdventure to choose
from print, audio or ebook. Alternatively contact
the author at arhetheringtonbooks@gmail.com

Copyright © 2020 by A. R. Hetherington

FIRST EDITION

www.arhetherington.com

About the Author

The author spent several years in Africa growing up and it is here that she first developed her love of reading due to there being no TV or other technology.

Her dad would tell her and her sister stories every week on their way back from their weekly visit to the library a couple of hours away. They were unique and creative stories which they both absolutely loved.

She has had all sorts of jobs over the years including horticulture, design and translation. For several years now she has been teaching primary school children part time as well as writing her fantasy adventures.

The author lives in a tiny rural village with her husband, lots of fancy hens and two mad spaniels called Rosie and Mabel. Her own boy and girl are grown up now and off creating adventures of their own.

For more information please visit her website at www.arhetherington.com

AR Hetherington

5

This book is dedicated to my two adorable fluffy, snuggly reading companions and my biggest fans of all, Rosie and Mabel; the best spaniels in the world!

THE SHANTY
REALM

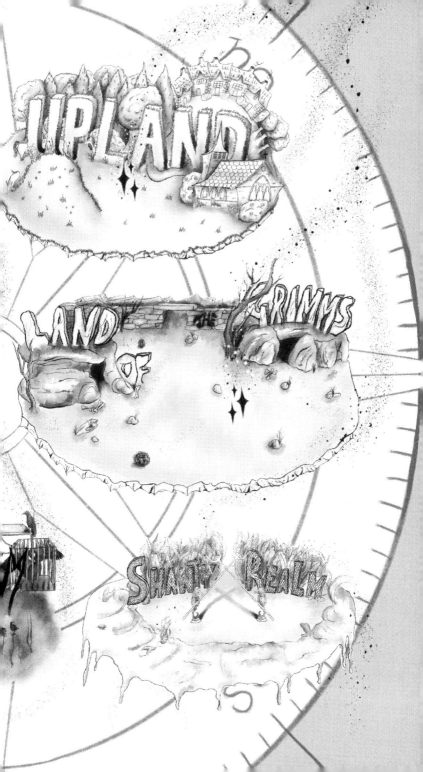

Contents

What Happened Next...

Maggie and Brocwulf stared at each other, neither made a move. Seconds ticked by, each waiting to see what the other would do. Finally Brocwulf glanced at Maggie's hands and so Maggie's eyes followed suit. There they were. The Alpha and Omega Rings, one on each hand. Maggie's whole body was tingling and fizzing with their combined power. She wondered, fleetingly, if it was safe for her to wear both of the rings. Maggie glanced at Storm, then raised her hands to look at the rings. Brocwulf took a step back, faltering slightly. Storm, her faithful companion still by her side, spoke into her mind.

11

"Maggie, I can't reach Jedrek; we have travelled far from the Earthlie Realm. I don't know this ocean place. Can you get rid of Brocwulf or are we all stuck here together?"

Jedrek was the companion of Wolfe, the Ancient of the school of Noble Beasts, and the two dogs could normally communicate with each other, even when not together. How far were they from their home Realm, Storm wondered?

Maggie glanced at her much loved puppy and then back at Brocwulf. Her eyes widened in alarm. Something was happening to Brocwulf. He appeared to be getting paler, not just his skin but everything; his hair, his eyes, his clothes. Brocwulf too looked down at himself as he caught the alarm in Maggie's gaze. He was starting to disappear! The Omega Ring he had worn for so many years had reduced the ageing process. But now, with the ring gone he was ageing at an alarming rate, shrinking and diminishing all at once. Then, as if every last drop of moisture had been sucked from his body leaving only desiccated skin and bones, he truly did begin to disintegrate. Like fine powder blown by the wind, Brocwulf simply blew away, little by little on the light breeze, until finally he was completely gone.

"That wasn't me Storm. That just happened by itself."

Storm nodded slowly. Either way, she was relieved. That was one less problem to solve. Now all they had to do was figure out where they were and how to get home. Maggie was thinking exactly the same thing. Plus, she was unsure what to do with the rings. Should she keep wearing them or take them off? She was scared that if she took them off she might lose them. That would be a disaster. Maggie wondered how the Earthlie Realm would fare without either ring. Would it be open to attack? Would the eco system start to break down? There was no time to lose. Maggie noticed that her thoughts were sharper and faster. Clearly the rings were having some sort of effect on her. Maybe they would help her figure out what to do.

"I'm hungry." Storm muttered.

Maggie smiled and nodded. Nothing like a bit of hunger to bring you back to reality. She was pretty hungry too now that she thought about it. She shrugged off her back pack which was thankfully none the worse for wear and rummaged around inside for provisions. She was able to produce a bag of dog biscuits, a box of Oat Floats, a few remaining Mores, a bottle of water and a flask of Elder fizzle. It didn't take long for the pair to feel restored. They decided to take stock of the situation by exploring their immediate surroundings. Storm kept trying to reach out to Jedrek and Maggie started to use her newly heightened senses to assess their immediate options.

Back in the Earthlie Realm

You could feel the tension all around, no one could escape the atmosphere of shock and disbelief. They had risked so much to gain the second ring and the cost of the battle had been high. But to go from the amazing success of seeing Maggie with the pair of rings together, to the horror of seeing her disappear with Brocwulf was hard to take in. Quinn, James, Vita and Archer had spent a lot of time together, gaining comfort from being close to each other, talking over different ideas and sharing news from their Ancients' discussions and meetings. James had, in between times, spent hours and hours pouring over books in the library and more hours

again discussing strategies with Madeline, his
Ancient, and Melville, his mentor. Quinn still felt
wretched that it was his banishing spell which had
so successfully sent not only Brocwulf, but Maggie
too, beyond the known Realm. If only she hadn't
reached forward at that very moment, if only she
hadn't been engulfed by his spell, if only Brocwulf
hadn't grabbed her and taken her with him. What
was done was done, however, and with a huge effort
Quinn had pulled himself out of his wallowing in
regret and set his mind to the task ahead. He had
also spent hours with his Ancient, Zephyr, trying to
extend the range of The Tracker to get an idea of
where Maggie, Brocwulf and Storm had ended up.

The small group from The School of Noble Beasts,
Maggie's school, were quite shaken by their loss of
Maggie and none more so than Vince and Selene.
Vince was the loyal Alpaca from the Grimms Realm
who had yet to return to The Snug, his group of
Alpacas, as he couldn't bear to leave the Earthlie
Realm without seeing Maggie home safely. Like all
animals, Vince was usually able to communicate

with Maggie telepathically, and he was deeply
distressed that there was silence in his mind in the
place where he normally was able to chat away with
his friend. Unlike other animals, Vince was able to
talk, a feature which made him all the more
endearing to the other children. He was normally an
over enthusiastic and rather confident creature, full
of bluster and tall stories; and it saddened them to
see him looking so forlorn and uncharacteristically
quiet. Selene too was distressed but she channelled
this emotion into constant pacing and pawing of the
ground, ever alert and ready for action. This
powerful and regal Goigil had a strong bond with
Maggie too, but only with Maggie. At times Selene
seemed quite aloof, rather haughty and more than a
little disparaging of Vince's antics. The pair had,
however, forged something of a friendship in
previous quests and were united in wanting to find
their dear companion.

Vita and Archer had been kept busy by their own
Ancients and schools. Vita was needed by Airmid,
The Ancient from the School of Herbs and Healing,

21

to help heal the wounded. Archer, along with the other Protectors, led by their Ancient Liath, had to ready themselves for the next potential attack. The Earthlies were all too aware that with neither ring in the Realm they were in an extremely vulnerable position. Keithia, the Principal Ancient and Leader of the School of Nature and Nurture was kept busy night and day assessing potential breaches to their security. The Alpha Ring, which she had guarded for many generations, had helped to keep the Realm's ecosystem in balance. The Omega Ring ensured prosperity and harmony and protection against evil. Not only were they now open to attack from the Grimm's Realm and also other Realms further away, but the careful balance of all that kept their realm fruitful and lush would soon start to break down. Before long the animals and birds would struggle to find enough food, as would the Earthlies themselves. There was absolutely no time to lose, they had to find Maggie, and find her fast. It was imperative that they launch a quest to bring her home. But where to start?

It was James who came up with the first idea. He had taken in a huge amount of information from books, maps and old manuscripts and had discussed many legends, theories and witness statements with Madeline and Mel. By twilight on the third day after Maggie and Storm had disappeared, he walked into the clearing more purposefully than usual to meet Quinn, Vita and Archer for their daily catch up. With uncharacteristic boldness, James called their attention to make an announcement.

"There might be a way to find them," he began, "there are old legends which tell of a far off group of people who live in water, or perhaps above water, or even on islands surrounded for miles and miles by water. It became known as The Shanty Realm on account of the people's reputed musical talents. It was long thought to be merely a myth, but my research has revealed common stories from a wide range of sources over the years, too many to be a coincidence. The Realm is deemed to be a great distance, even further than the furthest reported Realms. However, if Quinn's spell cast the three

23

beyond the known Realms, there is a chance that
The Shanty Realm may be a good starting point."

Silence followed this revelation as each of the group
pondered what this might mean. Quinn immediately
thought of adjustments he could make to The
Tracker, Vita thought of the new biological samples
that could be found and brought home from a new
Realm and Archer wondered if he would need to
consider underwater weapons for such a Realm.
Again James broke into their thoughts.

"The tricky bit, I imagine, is getting there. There are
secret links between our library here, and other
libraries in Realms below ground, as well as some
in Upland. Not everyone can access these links, a
bit like not everyone can conjure up portals like
Quinn. But I feel confident about it. I'm sure I can
find a way."

They all stared at James. They could hardly believe
their ears. None of them had ever heard of people
travelling through secret library passages between

Realms, and almost as surprisingly, they had never heard James sound so confident. Amazing!

"Right then," Quinn spoke for the others, "what are we waiting for? We need to find Keithia and the other Ancients and get a plan together. Meet you back here as soon as we can?"

The others all nodded as they watched Quinn stride out of the clearing with renewed determination in his steps and they soon followed suit.

CHAPTER 3

The First Secret Passageway

They discussed their plan with the Ancients, stocked up their equipment and were soon on their way. James led Quinn, Vita and Archer deeper into the library, concentrating on bringing up a mind boggling series of levels and connecting corridors. His three friends were utterly disorientated, but James strode forward with determination. Ancient book shelves loomed high on either side of them; clearly they were in a very old part of the library which was rarely visited. Thick dust coated every book and the atmosphere itself seemed heavy and untouched as they pushed their way forward. The others found the library oppressive, being used to an outdoor life in the fresh air, and the deeper they went the more uneasy they felt.

Finally, James stopped at what appeared to be a dead end. They were in a poorly lit side room with floor to ceiling shelving and no natural light. Cobwebs hung heavily from every nook and cranny and the floor boards creaked ominously as they shuffled to a stop behind him.

"Here we are," announced James. "So, if I'm right, and I think I am, this room links us to a room in The Library of Congress."

The others looked at him in amazement but also none the wiser for this additional information.

"You know, the largest library in the world, located in Washington DC in the United States of America?"

"James, if you mean we are going back to Upland then let's do it, but the one and only time we have been there before, was to a forest and a tiny village in England. America is surely the other side of the Upland planet?", checked Quinn looking a little baffled.

"Correct. The library itself is the national library of the United States and I think that is where we may get our next clue. I have reason to believe that there are librarians there who are part of the library. What I mean is, they are not normal librarians like the ones we know, rather they magically exist through all of the library's time and history and help protect the passages and secrets of the inter-library worlds above and below ground."

Archer and Vita looked to Quinn for reassurance. James' words hadn't made much sense to them but Quinn nodded at James, seemingly on board with this information.

"How do we get there then? Do I need to create a portal?" Quinn enquired.

"Not this time, I have been entrusted with a special universal library key by Madeline to use on this quest."

James reached into his shirt front and withdrew a long thin elaborate looking key which dangled from a silver chain around his neck.

"All we have to do is find the key hole, which is undoubtedly cloaked by magic. Quinn, that would be your department. See if you can detect where it is. Meanwhile we can just start looking."

James motioned for Vita and Archer to each take a shelf on different sides of the room. Clouds of dust and cobwebs soon filled the room as they pulled books off shelves in search of the secret key hole. Quinn stood stock still, eyes closed, reaching out with his magical senses. He had detected cloaking devices in every part of the library and it was a matter of sifting through the many different possible reveal spells, gradually discounting them one by one. He pushed harder, feeling the library pushing back and he staggered slightly under the sheer effort of maintaining his concentration. Vita glanced at her brother feeling anxious for him, but she knew how far he had come in his education over the past months and she was confident that if anyone could crack the spell, it would be him. It was beginning to seem a hopeless and pointless task moving yet more books - surely a cloaking spell would mean they wouldn't see the key hole even if they uncovered it? Quinn's eyes blinked open and he pointed to the wall immediately opposite him.

"It's right there, straight in front of me. I could feel the strong pull of the magic but there were heavy distracting spells that worked extremely well. I just couldn't get my mind to believe what I knew to be true. It's there though, I'm sure of it. Give me a minute."

Quinn muttered the appropriate reveal spell and held his hands up facing the bookshelves in front of them. Sure enough the shelves slid silently apart to the right and left, tucking themselves away to unveil a heavy wooden door and lock. James took

31

the key from around his neck and stepped forward slowly, ready to insert it. He paused and turned to the others.

"It's decision time. I won't blame you if you choose not to come. I could go through, find out what I can and report back. We don't know where we will end up in the library and who we will meet. Much of it is private and heavily guarded with security systems and a lot of technology."

"We're coming with you." Quinn spoke for the others and they nodded in unison. "Maggie is our friend too and we can all use our skills to help. Lead the way James."

They all held their breath as James nodded in response and inserted the key. It slipped effortlessly into the lock and James turned the key with little fuss. A series of clicks could be heard as if one lock unlocked another and another and another, until finally there was silence. With a quick glance back at the others, James centred his hands on the door

33

and pushed it open, firmly but slowly. There were no creaks, no dust, no surprises, nothing but a polished wood panelled passage way stretching out ahead of them. So far, so good. They trooped forward passing into the other side, one at a time. Quinn was thinking that there should surely be a little more fanfare to accompany this extraordinary feat of time travel but no, the only sound that could be heard was their footsteps echoing faintly in the corridor. Several tense moments passed as the group reached a turn in the passageway and paused to consider their options. Should they head right or carry straight on? Just then, louder footsteps could be heard coming towards them from the right. Breaking into a run, the four sped as quietly as they could down the passageway ahead until they breathlessly stumbled headlong into a magnificent lofty hallway; complete with marbled mosaic floors and highly decorative ceiling panels.

"The Great Hall!" James sounded awed as he gazed around, drinking in all the glory of the architecture and decoration that he had only previously been able to see online. "We actually made it! We're here, right in the Library of Congress. I can't believe it!"

James spoke reverently and quietly but with great passion.
"I thought you said you were confident James!" Quinn challenged playfully.
"Well, yes but knowing and doing are a bit different from believing and seeing!"

Archer had immediately adopted his surveillance mode, checking for incoming threats, traps and attacks. Vita too was feeling quite out of her comfort zone and shuffled a little closer to her friend Archer.

"Quinn." Archer called his attention. "A cloaking defence right now would be really useful."

Quinn nodded and with a sweep of his hands, covered all four of them in the now familiar cloaking bubble. They could see out but no one would be able to see in. At least, Uplanders would not. Librarians with magical skills might not be so easily fooled. Daylight had just broken and the hall became brighter, as sunlight shone in through the high windows. The four took stock of their situation. None of them could afford to relax for a second, not least because they knew already that there were others in the library, perhaps even security guards at this time of day. James hoped they hadn't been captured on CCTV before the cloaking spell had covered them and scolded himself inwardly for being momentarily distracted by the grandeur of the magnificent building. What was done was done however; time to come up with a plan. On the one hand they didn't want to be found, but on the other they did need to locate a magic librarian to help them find the clues necessary to get to the Shanty Realm. James paused for a moment to wonder how his good friend Maggie was doing.

Exploring the Shanty Realm

At that precise moment Maggie and Storm were staring at a creature making its way towards them. They were absolutely spell bound. What had appeared to be a mermaid swimming into the shallows one moment, had transformed into a beautiful girl who was smiling at them as she approached. She walked slowly and gracefully, her long fair hair, which held a tint of green in the sunlight, streamed water behind her.

"Hello new friends." The girl greeted them, smiling.

Maggie instantly felt uncharacteristically nervous. She tried to shake it off; clearly this girl was being

37

friendly and she certainly looked kind, but a little
shiver travelled up her spine.

"You must tell me all about yourself and your
journey. What brings you here?"

Storm uttered a barely audible whimper but Maggie
slowly rose to her feet. What else could they do?
They were far from home, far from their friends, far
from any sort of contact. Plus, she was conscious of
the Alpha and Omega rings constantly sending a
buzzing energy through her system. Yes, she needed
to rest and gather her thoughts and come up with a
plan. So, Maggie nodded and smiled again.

"To be honest we are really tired, it's so kind of you
to welcome us, we would love to rest. Tell us about
your Realm, Lana, it's absolutely beautiful. Did you
swim in? I honestly thought you were a mermaid
until you came on shore, crazy I know, I'm
probably more tired than I realise!"

Lana's sea green eyes flared brightly then darkened

momentarily.

"Your eyes did not deceive you. I am one of the Finfolk. There are many of us in our Realm. This is the Shanty Realm."

Maggie's gaze rested thoughtfully on Lana. She had read about Finfolk and Selkies in a book on Scottish mythology from the school library but surely that was just myth and legend? Interesting. Maggie wished James was with her, he would know every conceivable Finfolk fact available from every possible legend from every possible culture around the world. All that she could remember right now was that selkies could take on human form when they came on shore by shedding their seal skins. As for mermaids, she had honestly thought they did not truly exist, surely they were in the same category as unicorns and fairies?

Maggie just nodded and smiled. Her instincts warned her not to give away too much whilst learning as much about Lana and her Realm as she could.

39

"My mother's name is Hilda and we come from Finfolkaheem." Lana's eyes again took on a faraway look, but just as quickly she seemed to catch herself and beamed at Maggie.

"Come, I mustn't weary you with my story, I have a cabin nearby with a comfortable bed, fresh water and fruit, you will be quite safe."

Maggie and Storm walked by Lana's side. Maggie hadn't lied. It really was a beautiful Realm with exquisite turquoise seas surrounding the finest soft white sand on the shore, which gave way to tropical palms interspersed with beach huts on stilts. In the distance Maggie could see some of the Shanty folk going about their day; some were sitting on small boats on the shore mending nets, others were gathered in small groups engrossed in some sort of craft work or jewellery making. A small number of children splashed in the shallow waters or swam in and around seals. It was mesmerising. Lana indicated the nearest cabin.

"This cabin is for our guests. Make yourself at home, rest, eat and I will come back later this afternoon. I will bring my mother to greet you too."

"Thank you." Maggie smiled genuinely this time. She really was grateful to have found refuge. She and Storm climbed the steps wearily and walked through a doorway constructed from beautiful shells strung on long strings which clinked prettily as they swung together. Maggie heaved a sigh of relief as she entered a simple but beautiful cabin. There was little inside; a bed with invitingly clean white sheets and pillows, a low table made from drift wood with cream cushions either side, a bowl of tropical fruit and a jug of fresh water. There was no glass in the wide, low windows which framed breathtaking views on every side. A gentle breeze wafted through carrying the scent of sea salt. Storm instantly jumped onto the bed and, after circling a couple of times, settled down with a sleepy snuffle. Maggie poured herself a glass of water, drank deeply and then joined Storm, curling herself around her faithful companion. Within minutes they were both fast asleep, lulled by the sound of distant waves breaking onto the heavenly shores.

Sometime later Maggie woke with a start. She was initially disorientated, but as she adjusted to her surroundings every instinct was on full alert. There, reclining on the cushions, were Lana and the most intimidating and highly decorated woman Maggie had ever seen. Her long hair was the colour of stormy seas and settled in dishevelled waves around her shoulders and tumbled almost to her waist. There were shells of every imaginable colour and shape woven through this impressive mane. Her dress was unusual too; a fitted bodice covered in yet more tiny shells, sewn on by what looked like seaweed in many different colours. The sleeves appeared to be made from fishermen's nets, and her skirts seemed to ripple in all the colours of the oceans; from exquisite turquoise to a deep charcoal grey. Bangles jingled on her arms and all manner of shell necklaces adorned her neck. Most striking of all were her eyes; they were piercing and yet seemed to swirl like sea mist. Storm lifted her head

briefly then lay down again snuggling closer to Maggie, covering one eye with a huge paw. This must be Hilda, Lana's mum. She looked like some sort of Queen.

Hether Blether

Maggie smiled cautiously and sat up, leaning forward.

"Where am I? Where are we?"

It was the woman who spoke:

"The name of this enchanted island is Hether Blether, part of the Shanty Realm. You have already met my daughter Lana. I'm Hilda. I am the leader of our people here. You are welcome, both of you."

She glanced at Storm.

"No other dogs live here and it's been a very long time since I've seen one but I'm sure we can

49

provide for her."

Maggie nodded thoughtfully. She was sure the name Hether Blether rang a distant bell in her mind, it was such an unusual name you would hardly forget it. Something from Scottish folklore perhaps, but this island was certainly tropical and not like Scotland in the slightest with its palms and the warm air. Maggie waited for Hilda to speak again. This formidable looking lady seemed to be assessing her.

"So, tell me a bit about yourself then Maggie. Not often we get unexpected visitors here. You've come all the way from the Earthlie Realm Lana tells me.

"I'm not really sure how we got here. It was a mistake I think." This part was truthful. "Our people were sending someone else away, far away, and somehow I got entangled in the spell."

"And this other person?"

"Gone, they're not here." Maggie was reluctant to

mention Brocwulf by name.

"You possess great magic. I can sense it. The rings I think?" Hilda nodded to Maggie's hands and Maggie instinctively curled her hands into fists.

"I'm looking after them, that's all. I need to take them back, straight away. The Earthlie Realm needs them. Do you know how we can get back?"

"Well, dear, all in good time. I will help you both return. For now, though, I think you should put the rings on this chain and secure it around your neck. Much safer. Those rings seem a bit loose on your fingers. You don't want to lose such precious objects now that you are guardian to them."
Hilda held out a chain which she had taken from around her neck. Wordlessly Maggie took it and did as she had said. It seemed sensible, the rings were indeed a bit loose, imagine if they came off and got lost in the sand or in the sea. She would never forgive herself. It would be an utter disaster for the Earthlie Realm.

"Come now, my lovely ones. Come and meet my Finfolk and the Selkies. We have prepared some food. Then Lana can give you a tour and help you get settled in. There is no rush, no rush at all."

Maggie stood as she secured the chain over her head and tucked it inside her top. Storm followed as they made their way slowly down the steps of the cabin and across the beach. Maggie suddenly felt like a huge weight had been lifted from her shoulders and she heaved a sigh of relief. The rings seemed to have calmed too, and the energy levels that they had been pulsing through her became gradually less. The buzz was much gentler; she hardly noticed it now at all. It really was a beautiful place here she noticed again, almost hypnotised by the beautiful surroundings.

Storm cocked her head to one side and gazed thoughtfully at Maggie. Something unusual was happening here and she wasn't sure it was a good thing. Storm didn't trust Hilda or Lana, not one bit. There was something definitely sinister about

53

this island and she needed to persuade Maggie that they should escape as soon as they could. Little did Storm know how right she was. Hilda was not at all a kind woman and she had no intention of letting Maggie leave soon or indeed ever. This enchanted isle had a complicated and dangerous history lurking beneath its beauty.

The Librarian

Meanwhile, back in the Library of Congress, Quinn took the lead. James had done a brilliant job getting them there but Archer and he were used to being out in the field. As quietly as possible they checked each room systematically, Quinn searching for any hint of magic and Archer on the lookout for incoming attacks. Vita and James found it hard to do anything but gaze admiringly at the wonderful architecture and books. They soon came across the main reading room where it was almost impossible to move as a four, due to the layout of the desks in widening circles around a central station. Quinn dropped the cloaking bubble so they could fan out more easily.

"Well, well, well." A dry, whispering voice rustled across the domed area. "This is an honour and no mistake. It's been a very, very long time since I've had visitors here. Decades I believe, maybe more. Welcome to my library."

Their four pairs of eyes scanned the room. Where was that voice coming from? Then, slowly, ever so slowly, a figure started to reveal itself, appearing gradually, materialising from nothing but coming into focus right before their eyes. An extremely elderly man was standing in the central desk area. Old but upright, with a twinkle in his grey eyes.

"My name is Benjamin. Whom do I have the pleasure of meeting?"

Quinn stepped forward, recognising that this was the sort of introduction that involved hand shaking and not just a casual 'hi'. He made the necessary introductions and nodded to James to step forward.

"Young man," Benjamin fixed him with a direct look. "How may I be of service to you? I would reason that you are not just here to view a manuscript; fellow librarians who travel through our secret passageways invariably have something of the utmost importance about which they are seeking advice. Am I right?"

James nodded, rather pleased at being hailed as a fellow librarian. He explained what had happened, with the others chipping in with him as they saw fit. Benjamin did not interrupt once and listened intently, with an increasingly serious look clouding his eyes. A long silence followed their recount of events.

"Come," he said finally. "It's time to introduce you to a couple of friends. This is going to take a bit of team work. Follow me, you will be quite safe, we can pass undetected. We have our own secret passageways within the library."

With that Benjamin walked, with surprising vigour,

towards a plinth on top of which one of the mighty columns reached up to the arched windows and domed ceiling. He tapped out a combination on the stone causing a section of it to swing inward. The four friends traipsed after him, curious to find out where the secret passageway would lead. James was surprised. He had expected it to be dark and musty but there were light boxes along the passage which reminded him of those in the Earthlie Realm. As if reading his mind, Benjamin turned and smiled at him.

"We're quite progressive these days, you know? Plenty of time to read up on all the latest inventions. Keep up now, nearly there."

It was hard, even for Archer, to keep track of the twists and turns they took. Were they going up or down? After several more minutes Benjamin reached another door. It looked solid and heavy, made of wood. Benjamin pushed it open with unexpected ease and it swung back on well-oiled hinges to reveal a very cosy, much smaller, reading room with a burning fire. In fact, it looked like a cross between an old English country pub and a tea room. There were comfortable armchairs, on which were seated some elderly gentlemen similar to Benjamin, a range of tables covered in papers, cups and saucers, but in place of a bar there were long rows of books from floor to ceiling.

"Though of course it's still important we enjoy a few old fashioned comforts." Benjamin commented over his shoulder to James.

"Alexander, Tolly, Robert, Edward, we have young visitors! Make some room and let's get the kettle on shall we? We have mportant things to discuss."

The four elderly men creaked and shuffled as they stood to their feet, stepping forward to shake the hands of their unexpected visitors. Cups of tea were shortly circulated, along with a welcome plate of jaffa cakes and oreos. James was familiar with both types of biscuit and tucked in heartily, the others were a little warier of the Upland offerings but

60

soon followed suit, nodding appreciatively. James rummaged in his back pack and brought out a bag of snacks which he offered to the gentlemen.

"Try these. Mores from the Earthlie Realm, and Oat Floats too. Absolutely delicious." More munching and appreciative murmurs, this time from the librarians. Finally they settled down to discuss the urgent matter at hand. Benjamin summarised the situation and his colleagues leaned forward with their intelligent eyes fixed firmly on him. Excitement, interest and a little unease seemed to shine out from their faces.

"Well now." Tolly spoke up. "I admire your nerve and loyalty young travellers, but a dangerous quest is ahead of you. The outer Realm of which Benjamin talks is a wicked and cunning place. Very few have made it there and even fewer return. Travellers pass through our library from time to time and we record all their adventures. We have heard of islands which appear and disappear in distant oceans; inhabited by strange beings and creatures. It may be that young Quinn has summoned enough magic to banish this Brocwulf and your friends to these far flung shores. If so, I must warn you that they are not safe, not safe at all. Take heart though, we will tell you everything we know, but it is vital you act quickly, there is not a moment to lose. I fear your friend and her companion are in the gravest of dangers. And if you do reach their shores, there is no guarantee you will return."

Finfolk and Selkies

It was Robert who then told the tale of the mythical creatures who were reported to be living in the Shanty Realm.

"You will hear different versions of these folk, but what I tell you is the truest record put together from Traveller's stories over the years. It is for you to decide what you believe and perhaps discover for yourselves. The Finfolk can take human form on shore at will, as well as being mermen and mermaids in the ocean. Selkies are seals in the ocean and shed their skins as they come ashore to take on human form, many say they are kinder than

63

the Finfolk.

There is a city in the deepest part of the ocean called Finfolkaheem which the Finfolk are extremely proud of. They spend much time there in the winter when the seas are at their stormiest. It is reputed to be of an unparalleled beauty with tall white columns of coral embedded with pearls and jewels, along with crystal halls and magnificent gardens full of multi-coloured seaweed. The Finfolk spend their time hunting for treasures to adorn their ancestral home and you will have heard many a story of them conspiring to sink ships in order to gain precious items to take home. They keep magical sea horses and herd sea cattle and whales from which they get their milk. These magical creatures lure and trap mortals on their vanishing island to inter-marry with their kind. If they marry a human, they may stay on shore in human form for ever and this is why there are many stories of human kind simply disappearing over the years, never to be seen again. It is said that the longer mortals stay on the island the more they forget themselves and their history. Some say they are hypnotised or that the leader casts an enchanting spell to make them forget their home and any desire to escape. This may be why few Travellers return from these far flung shores and this is why we fear for your friends and for you too."

"Thank you for the warning." Quinn spoke up, "but the decision has already been made, and we must get ready to move on as soon as we can. Maggie and Storm are obviously in great danger."

"If you are sure, then we cannot stop you. Let me give you a copy of a map we have drawn up." Edward unrolled a piece of parchment from a collection piled higgledy-piggledy on a table beside him. "This is the best we can do for now, but perhaps on your return you may have information to add?" He smiled in a kindly way at each of the children. Archer and Vita stepped forward to look more closely at the map.

"One more thing." Robert added. "If, or indeed when, the Finfolk find out that you are on their island and trying to help your friends escape, they

65

will use all their power to trap you and if that fails, to drown you. They can conjure up the fiercest of storms and they ride their seahorses like the wind."

Benjamin smiled encouragingly at the children. "Now then, one step at a time. I will prepare a letter for you to take to Kai, a fellow librarian. She is our contact in Hawaii's library in their capital city of Honolulu. Kai will be able to advise you on how best to proceed but that is as far West as the library network goes. From there you will be relying on your wits and skills, along with magic of course. Tolly will prepare food for the journey; Alexander will gather a few useful items and Edward will write down notes about the Finfolk which might come in handy. I think an hour should do it."

With that Benjamin sat down at an ancient writing bureau and picked up a magnificent fountain pen ready to prepare their letter of introduction. True to his word, within an hour all the provisions were assembled and the children were poised ready to be led through another secret passageway to the

66

Hawaii library portal. All four were feeling a jumble of emotions; excitement and fear mixed in with a hefty dose of adrenaline. Time to take the next step in their quest to rescue Maggie and Storm.

Maggie and Storm

A group of Finfolk and Selkies in their human form were gathered around a beach fire; some were cooking and chatting, but as they approached a hush descended and all eyes turned toward Hilda.

"Let me introduce our guests, Maggie and Storm. I know you will welcome them and make them feel at home here. For now, though, they are hungry and thirsty. Let us celebrate their arrival and all that it means to our humble community."

Murmurings and shuffling started up as the Finfolk and Selkies moved apart to allow the guests to sit nearer to the fire, which seemed to be a central point for the community. Plates of roasted vegetables and toasted seeds were swiftly produced though Storm wasn't entirely convinced this would be a filling meal. Clearly she would have to make do for now and she started to chew on a corn cob whilst eyeing the crowd warily. Storm tried to project her concerns into Maggie's mind but Maggie seemed distracted and merely gave her a half-hearted pat as she looked around, eyes slightly glazed.

Lana and another mermaid who was called Galia, sat by Maggie; Lana made sure her plate was kept full and Galia stroked her arms and hair, starting to plait it, adding little shells and pearls and seaweed threads. Maggie smiled at them both, she really felt happy and relaxed. As the sun set and they all finished their meal the Finfolk started to sing in haunting, lilting voices. The songs told of their history, songs of the oceans, songs full of joy and heartache; sea shanties from all parts of the world. Maggie wasn't sure when she fell asleep but the next thing she knew she awoke to find herself in a cabin. She could tell from the dark sky and the twinkling stars that it was very late. As her eyes adjusted to the gloom she instinctively reached out her hand to Storm but the bed was strangely quiet and empty. No little snores or snuffles could be heard, no warm presence to reassure her. Maggie sat bolt upright with a start. Storm wasn't there. She reached up to her neck. The chain was missing. The rings were gone! The fogginess that had been in her mind earlier that evening had completely evaporated. Maggie was frightened. What had happened? What had she done? Where were the rings? She reached out in her mind for Storm and with some relief she sensed their bond, though it seemed much more fragile than before. Storm was still on the island, that much was sure but she seemed to be unreachable. Was she asleep, was she unconscious? She could also sense that she wasn't alone in the cabin. Sure enough the silently sleeping forms of Lana and Galia could just be made out on another bed opposite. Could she escape without waking them? Maggie took a tentative step toward the door, then another and another. With her breath held tightly in her chest she reached the curtained

71

doorway and stretched out her hand to part the shells. Impossible! No sooner had her fingers brushed the shells than they tinkled prettily, raising the alarm.

"Can we help you?" The girls cooed in unison.

"Just looking for Storm." Maggie smiled, her heart beating so loudly she was sure they could hear it.

"Oh, she's fine. Fast asleep in a special cabin we got ready just for her. We aren't used to dogs and we knew you wouldn't mind. This is our cabin you're sharing. Come back to bed now, it's time to sleep."

As they reached out their hands and interlinked their fingers with hers, Maggie started to feel drowsy and calm again. After all, it was the middle of the night. No need to disturb Storm if she was safely sleeping, there was plenty of time to find her in the morning. She yawned and lay down beside Galia, Lana taking the other bed. The girls exchanged glances and Galia tucked her arm around Maggie's waist pulling

72

her in close.

Maggie slept fitfully. She was restless and her dreams were unsettled with confusing pictures and memories of others gliding through them. Were they friends or people she had met somewhere? Who was James, she thought she should know him? Storm was in her dreams along with some children, other creatures too. Who was Vince? Did she really know an alpaca? She tossed and turned with Galia stroking her hair and Lana singing soft lullabies to calm her. As dawn slipped her fingers through the windows and tickled her eyelids, Maggie's dreams turned to the rings. Were they hers, had she lost them? Despite the confusion in her mind she awoke knowing that she had to find these rings. They were extremely valuable and important, that much she knew. She had to find them. She slipped gently out from Galia's embrace and climbed silently through the window; both mermaids were finally fast asleep. It was time to find Storm.

CHAPTER 9

Trapped

Storm paced restlessly in a caged off area beneath a stilted beach hut. She was furious and ashamed; she had been tricked! One of the mermen, Finn, had come up beside her whilst Maggie slept by the fire and whispered that he had a proper meal for her and they could take a walk while Maggie rested. She should have known not to leave her companion's side and now she was trapped. Finn and another merman, Jonas, had indeed walked with her along the beach some distance and then guided her into the caged area where there was a big bowl of tempting food. Just like that she had been trapped as the mermen closed a gate behind her and secured it strongly. They had looked a little apologetic and indicated some water and a blanket for Storm. Clearly they were following orders and they headed back to the finfolk.

Where was Maggie? Storm could still sense her, though their link was tenuous and foggy. Hilda was surely casting some kind of hypnotic spell over Maggie; the selkies were in on it too, she just knew it. They were making her forget who she was and what her purpose here was. Storm suspected Hilda was after the rings; she hadn't been able to keep her eyes off them and it was she who had persuaded Maggie to put them on a chain around her neck as soon as they got here. That alone seemed to allow Hilda's magic to start to take effect as the ring's powers of protection lessened somewhat. What if Hilda got hold of them? What would she do? What would become of the Earthlie Realm and where were the others? Storm knew they would be on their way somehow but time was marching on. They needed a rescue and they needed it soon. She paced even more uneasily back and forth and then came to a standstill. She heard a noise, some scuffling, and then as clear as day, Maggie's voice. Storm's ears pricked up and then flattened and a growl escaped from her, her hair standing on end.

"Let me go!" Maggie demanded, "I just want to find Storm. What's going on? Where are my rings? You can't keep us here!"

"It's for your own good." Finn's voice tried to calm her, "I am taking you to Storm but you should not have been out looking for her, Hilda will be angry. We're leaving today anyway and we are taking you with us."

"Leaving? What do you mean? Is Storm coming too?"

"You will see. No, Storm can't come where we are going. You can say your goodbyes here."

With that Finn opened the gate and pushed Maggie gently but firmly into the cage. She immediately hugged Storm tight, fussing her ears and checking

her all over. Their connection strengthened with their contact and they quickly exchanged details of the last few hours. There were lots of apologies on both sides, tight cuddles and a few tears on Maggie's part. What would become of them? What would happen to Storm when they left her here? Maggie shook herself and tried to gather her wits and her nerve. She needed to be strong for Storm. She knew the others would be on their way to rescue them, but how on earth would they find them? She still had little idea of where they were. Was it a magic Realm? Could it move or disappear? Maggie didn't have long to wait. She heard a noise and looked up to see Hilda, flanked by Lana and Galia on one side and Finn and Jonas on the other side, heading toward them.

"Well then. I had hoped to do this a little more smoothly but you give me no option," she addressed Maggie, "You need to come with us to Finfolkaheem, our city. I want to offer these rings to our Queen in exchange for my freedom. We leave at once. Your dog can't come; the journey is deep below the waves. She will be safe here and my people will feed her."

"What do you mean deep below the waves?" Maggie asked alarmed, "I can't do that, I don't have diving equipment, I will never survive that journey."

Hilda smiled, and in that smile Maggie could read her history; one of pain, sadness and betrayal. Perhaps she did have kindness in her heart once but she clearly had been wronged and badly hurt and this harshness had taken over. What had happened to her? Maggie could understand the desire for freedom all too clearly in her current situation. Fear and alarm were bubbling up again and Maggie struggled to keep calm.

"The girls will help you," Hilda continued, nodding at the finfolk, "we have our ways of getting you mortals down safely. It is the coming up which is usually trickier but who knows if that will even happen."

With those chilling words Hilda indicated for the mermen to release Maggie, who barely had time to give Storm a last hug. Storm whimpered and clawed at the gate but it was locked firmly again and she could only watch helplessly as Maggie was led away; Galia and Lana linking her arms on each side, casting their hypnotic spell again through their physical contact with her. Storm howled; the most mournful and pitiful sound that she had never made.

CHAPTER 10

Below the Sea

Hilda led the way directly towards the shore line. Maggie felt calm again with the finfolk by her side; she suddenly couldn't remember why she had been so upset just moments before. She was looking forward to a swim, the girls wanted to show her some lovely things out at sea. What could be better? As the waves started to reach her feet she smiled, how warm, how inviting it felt. She walked on, relishing the feel of the water on her calves and then her thighs. She glanced to one side, eyes widening as the mermen's legs changed before her, iridescent scales where once there had been smooth skin.

85

Long, lithe tails flicked and swished and the girls were now sleek beautiful mermaids. As her toes left the sea bed Galia and Lana guided her along easily, further and further from the shore. Soon the beach was a thin slither of gold on the horizon and the deeper waves undulated gently around them. Hilda and the mermen swam strongly beside them. After a few more strokes, and as the beach disappeared completely from sight, Hilda nodded a signal.

"Take a breath," Hilda advised, "we're going down now."

Maggie drew in a deep breath and held it tightly as the group dived down deep with a last flick of their tails above the waves. Faster and faster they dived, deeper into the ocean, the sunlight twinkling on the surface further and further away. Maggie started to run out of breath and panic started to bubble up. What was she doing? She became light headed but couldn't struggle, she was being pulled strongly through the water and she had no energy of her own. As her mouth opened to take in the salty water

Hilda turned and brought her lips close to Maggie's. She breathed into Maggie causing Maggie's eyes to initially open in alarm but then just as quickly she felt calm again. It was like she could breathe easily now and see all around her; she smiled at Hilda and nodded her thanks. She looked keenly around now, able to take in her surroundings as their pace slowed a little.

They were descending into a deep valley within a vast coral reef. Her mind fluttered briefly over a distant memory of another much smaller reef, some turtles and some friends perhaps but it had been nothing compared to this. This reef was magnificent and stretched as far as the eye could see; a whole vast undersea landscape. There were hills and valleys and mountains, and as for the creatures, well Maggie drank in everything hungrily with her eyes. Words would never ever do them justice; the colours, the shapes, the varieties of incredible sea life. It was as if all the most wondrous and special sea creatures in the entire universe were living here; safe from trawlers, safe from plastic and pollution, safe from people. There were also forests and fields and jewel like flowers; all different types of seaweed and coral. Structures and plants towered above her as the sea bed came into view.

Maggie suddenly startled as she observed the scene below. They were not alone down here. Coming into focus were a crowd of finfolk. If Maggie had thought Hilda was intimidating, she instantly realised she had been nothing compared to the sea Queen before her now. Not only did she wear a magnificent coral crown with enormous pearls embedded in it, but her look was so striking with her haughty expression, wavy hair even longer than Hilda's and her magnificent jewelled tail. She commanded absolute authority.

As they came to a quiet stop on the sea bed, the finfolk, who Maggie could now see were guards, parted a little and the Queen swam gracefully forward. The others all bowed low and Maggie copied as best she could, feeling clumsy with her legs. Galia and Lana held out their hands to her.

Maggie held on and kept her balance in the ebb and sway of the ocean's currents.

Hilda spoke first.

"My Queen Merilla, we come respectfully into your presence and ask that you grant us an audience to offer you a gift of great value."

Queen Merilla regarded Hilda, a sneering expression on her face, and several moments passed before she inclined her head, granting Hilda permission to approach. Hilda swam forward but motioned for the others to stay where they were. Queen Merilla was regarding Maggie with some interest but her face gave little away.

"Gracious guardian of our oceans and Queen of the Shanty Realm," continued Hilda, "it has been some months since my last visit. An event of great importance has taken place on our island. Hether Blether has received a visitor, the first for many, many years. A visitor who has powers and bears rings containing potent magic; I have never come

90

across such valuable treasure in my lifetime. I bring you our visitor and I have the rings here too." At this Hilda indicated both Maggie with a nod of her head and the rings on the chain now secured around her own neck.

Queen Merilla did not speak. The silence lengthened forcing Hilda to carry on speaking: "I hope that my gift finds favour with you, my Queen. Do you wish to examine the treasure or our visitor? I humbly offer them to you that they might add to the matchless treasures of your magnificent Queendom." Hilda bowed low again and the finfolk followed suit.

Finally Queen Merilla responded by merely raising her hand and beckoning Maggie forward. Lana and Galia escorted her towards the Queen, heads bowed humbly as they approached. Queen Merilla gazed imperiously at Maggie, her eyes searching her, perhaps for clues, perhaps for treasure.
"Your name?" she finally commanded, her voice echoing out through the water.

"Maggie."

"You don't belong here, yet I am interested." Queen Merilla raised her trident and brought it down like a sword as if to knight her. As the trident touched her shoulder Maggie's feet became heavy and the mermaids retreated. Maggie stood up straight and tried out her new found gravity. She lifted first one foot and then the next, it felt strange - like moving in quicksand, but at least she didn't float away. The Queen gestured to some of her guards; powerful finfolk who unbelievably, now that Maggie's eyes had adjusted, sat astride stately seahorses. How beautiful they were, but their strong rippling muscles, on both sets of creatures, told Maggie not to mistake beauty for kindness. Maggie shook herself, unease creeping in again. Where was she? Queen Merilla held out her hand indicating that Hilda should pass her the rings. Maggie's eyes followed their exchange and a part of her brain suddenly lit up. The rings! Of course! They were hers, or at least they had been. Now why were they important? She racked her brains trying to shake her memories back into place. Suddenly she froze as it all flooded back to her and she gasped despite herself. All eyes swivelled towards her as Maggie's hand shot up to her mouth in shock at the sudden realisation of where she was and the danger she found herself in. Queen Merilla merely smiled as she twisted the rings this way and that, and finally turning to Maggie she announced:

"You're mine now and here you will stay. Forever." She turned to Hilda and continued, "You honour me with your gifts. I too will bestow a favour on you. What shall it be?"

"I request my freedom, if it pleases you? I wish to travel the oceans and find my husband and my children."

Queen Merilla pierced Hilda with her solemn gaze. "This is no small favour you ask. I am not sure I can spare you from guarding Hether Blether and bringing me trinkets, however, this is what I propose. "Your people", she indicated the finfolk who waited behind Hilda, " will continue to keep guard, but you must elect one to take your place. Choose wisely as you know all too well it is both an honour and a curse. Then you may have your freedom for a year. After that time, you must return and we will consider if I grant you more than that. It rather depends on my new treasures here and what I can do with them." She glanced again at the rings and then secured the chain around her neck.

"What is your decision?"

Hilda looked at all four of her finfolk and considered the matter. They did not know that they could leave Hether Blether right now if they chose to, she had cast her own spell on them to make them want to stay, but once she elected one to be her successor then there would be no escape. They would be under Queen Merilla's spell and spend years, decades even trying to earn their freedom. None of the four were yet married or had children of their own so that was a joy they may never know.

Hilda shook herself, she refused to allow kindness to creep back in at this point. This was her chance. She had been captured years ago when she had strayed into Queen Merilla's Realm, carelessly exploring. She had always been curious but had gone too far on that fateful occasion. Her husband, Taron, had seen it happen as he minded their girls, Ava and Lyra, allowing her some time to herself to explore this far off reef from their home. A whole legion of seahorses had sailed into view, the sea completely darkening and thrashing around them. Finfolk guards had grabbed hold of Hilda and the last thing she saw was the anguished look on her husband's and children's faces as she was dragged away; another gift for their Queen. How many years ago had that been? She had lost count. Her children would be grown up by now, how she longed to see them again, if only for a very last time. She made her choice.

"Finn, I choose you. Lana, Galia and Jonas you must help him. I will return in one year's time and then I promise to set you all free. This is my word."

96

Queen Merilla nodded her acknowledgement.
"Let it be so. Go now Hilda, have your time but be careful, I expect you back a year from now and not a moment later. Go!"

Hilda turned and with a powerful thrust of her tail she was gone in a swirl of bubbles.

What next, thought Maggie?

CHAPTER 11

To the Rescue

James, Quinn, Archer and Vita turned and waved to Benjamin as they passed through another doorway into the Hawaiian State Public Library, where an intelligent looking woman was smiling at them. She was medium height with long dark hair and her voice was welcoming:

"Aloha. Hello," she translated. She stretched out her hand to take the letter of introduction from James and scanned it keenly. Her expression clouded but she nodded and indicated with her hand for them to follow her. She walked quickly and the others sped up to keep up with her. Kai spoke rapidly, explaining as they hurried through the library and out through some tall, stately columns that they would need to catch a bus to Laniakea Beach; also known as Turtle Beach. That was really all she could tell them. There had been sightings of islands in the distance from that beach at times but not for many, many years. Quinn shook his head at this suggestion of travelling by bus, too public; he would create a portal. Kai nodded but pointed at her watch. Time to get going before the local community began their day.

Quinn spread his arms wide, concentrating on the name of the beach: Laniakea. He pictured turtles in his mind too, it wasn't much to go on but as it wasn't that far away it shouldn't be too tricky to reach it. What lay beyond was another matter. With surprising ease Quinn conjured a small, shimmering portal and the others dived through it quickly, waving a quick thank you to Kai as they passed her. Quinn too nodded his thanks before stepping through closing the portal with a flick of his hand. Kai shook her head as she returned to her duties in the library. It had been quite some time since travellers had come her way and she was grateful to be part of their journey, however small. She just hoped they would be able to reach their destination safely. She planned her response to Benjamin as she hurried back through the pillars. Her old friend and fellow librarian would be anxious to hear what had happened.

Meanwhile the others stepped out on to Laniakea Beach. Golden sands and palm trees greeted them, along with.....turtles! Two enormous turtles appeared right there in front of them. James smiled; he wished Maggie was here to explain that they could do with a bit of help. A shrill shriek caught their attention and they looked up simultaneously. Could that be Pontus and Thalassus? How did they get here? Sure enough, two magnificent sea eagles were circling high above their heads. These regal birds were friends of Maggie's and had helped transport them all from their own Turtle Bay in the Earthlie Realm back to their forest on a previous quest. How marvellous that they were here!

The eagles swooped down to the beach, landing a few metres away and bowed their heads low. The children did likewise, looking at each other and wondering what this could mean. Quinn took charge.

"I think they want to take us out to sea, come on, let's climb aboard."

Luckily it was still early enough that no locals were around as the eagles crouched low for the children's approach. Quinn and James gently climbed up on to Pontus' strong back while Vita and Archer climbed up on to Thalassus. With a few strong thrusts of their wings the eagles pushed hard with their legs and just like that they were airborne again. The beach soon became smaller and smaller, as did the whole island; they could see its entire outline, even the library momentarily. In seconds, they were far from shore travelling over the sea. Miles and miles of ocean lay below them as far as the eye could see, it truly was vast.

Sometime later the eagles came almost to a standstill; they hovered, trying to maintain their position whilst nodding their heads towards something below and gave their passengers a little shake. James looked at Quinn with alarm, were they going to be tipped off into the ocean with no land anywhere in sight? Quinn acted quickly, he balanced on Pontus' shoulders and stood carefully, arms stretched and concentrating with all his might. Not only did he need to keep steady but he wanted to create a protective bubble for them all to climb into. With a huge effort Quinn widened his arms in a circular swooping motion and flung his hands to one side. Sure enough a luminous bubble appeared, large enough to contain all four of them and he nodded his chin at it; indicating to the others that this was their next ride. Vita went first, leaping nimbly directly from Thalassus into the bubble. Archer followed but James shook his head, clearly terrified. Quinn grabbed him around the waist and Pontus angled steeply readying himself to fly off, and with that they part fell, part slipped, part tipped, straight into the bubble from above. Miraculously all four landed on their feet, wavering slightly; the inner surface was a bit like that of a trampoline. James cautiously opened his eyes then shut them again immediately, hunkering down, arms wrapped around his knees. Quinn shrugged at the others, he didn't know what to do but Vita knelt down beside him and put a reassuring hand on his shoulder.

"We're OK James", she whispered gently, "we're safe enough in here. We're going to float down and take a look."

James nodded but kept his eyes shut and his head tucked into his knees. Down they floated as gently as if they were in a hot air balloon on a calm day. Only a few minutes had passed before they were floating two or three metres above the calm ocean; it was so clear they could see several metres down into the turquoise waters. The bubble landed and they floated safely, as if in a boat.

"I think we're leaking Quinn." Archer spoke up. Sure enough water was definitely seeping through

the surface of the bubble where it was touching the water, causing James to open his eyes and stand up in panic. All four scanned the horizon, and as if in response, there before their very eyes and less than one hundred metres away, a beach, palm trees, land, huts, in fact a whole island started to rise up from beneath the ocean. Waves rippled out strongly towards them. That was the final straw; as the waves struck their bubble it popped, and all four were up to their necks as they dropped into the ocean.

"To shore", shouted Quinn as he struck out swimming toward the magically appearing island. He had definitely sensed magic very strongly around him but had not expected this. So it was true! There were disappearing islands. Tolly had been right. What luck, he hadn't thought they would actually be able to find one quite so soon, but was it actually the one where Maggie was? Time would tell. Soon all four were wading up through shallow waters, James bringing up the rear and they all flopped on to the sand to catch their breath. Quinn and Archer scanned the island for people or predators while Vita patted James firmly on the back, and he spluttered up a mouthful of sea water. Quinn could still sense magic but as to what kind he couldn't be sure.

"Let's fan out but stick together." Quinn ordered jumping to his feet, "we've got to find Maggie."

The children didn't know it at the time but another piece of luck had come their way. The finfolk were gathered on a beach on the other side of the island awaiting Hilda's return with her mermaids, therefore no one observed the children's arrival, nor did they notice as they searched the island looking for clues. Before too long the children were drawn towards Storm's cage where there was a delighted reunion amongst them. Storm licked James thoroughly, much to his discomfort, and the other three showered her in hugs and kisses. Luck has a habit of running out, however, and as the hairs on the back of Quinn's neck rose, warning him that danger approached, Jonas appeared from around the back of the hut. They had returned from

10

their journey and he had come to check on his captive. There was quite a standoff with Storm growling, hackles raised, whilst the merman and the children locked eyes; steely stares on both sides.

Finfolkaheem

"Where did you come from?" Jonas broke the impasse.

"We're here for Maggie, where is she?" Quinn demanded, ignoring the question.

Just then Finn, Galia and Lana appeared and the Earthlie children and James then watched spellbound as a furious debate broke out among the Finfolk. Finn had, of course, been chosen by Hilda to lead in her absence and with this honour, full realisation had come to him of the real story behind the island. He shared the startling information with the others that while all the finfolk were actually free to go if they chose to, Hilda had enchanted them to stay to help find treasures to give to Queen Merilla in order to try and win her favour and in turn secure her own freedom. Lana and Galia were clearly conflicted. On the one hand they felt betrayed, on the other hand Hilda had promised to return in a year and set them free. Were they free anyway? Would Finn let them go or would he also use his new found powers bestowed by Hilda to trap them too? Finn insisted he would not but neither did he want them to leave him. Jonas was furious; he wanted to leave straight away and clearly felt some guilt at Maggie being used as a pawn in Hilda's plan. The row continued with the finfolk demanding their freedom and threatening to tell the others until finally Quinn broke in:

"Help us find Maggie and in return we will help you all gain your freedom."

Silence followed as they all considered this proposal.

11

"How can we trust you?" Finn demanded.

"The same way we will have to trust you."

The long silence that followed this became tense and uncomfortable. Finally, Finn nodded his agreement.

"We act now and we tell no one. Let's move." This time, eight of them strode towards the shore, Finn and Quinn discussing plans.

Quinn gave a couple of orders to Vita and Archer to outline the part they would play and he cautioned James to stick close. James looked petrified but did as he was told, he didn't want to follow but he didn't want to stay here without them and he definitely was desperate to help to get Maggie back. When Storm followed them into the water, Finn rolled his eyes and told Jonas he would have to deal with the dog. Jonas nodded, a twinkle in his eye, there was a first time for everything after all. As before, they swam far out to sea, the finfolk turning

into their mer forms, astounding the children. Storm
paddled furiously with her paws, desperate not to be
left behind. Finn gave the instruction for them all to
hold their breath and they dived below the surface.
Storm was left at sea level, unsure what to do next.
Jonas quickly returned and placing his mouth beside
hers blew strongly into her lungs. Holding her by
the shoulders he dived down again. Incredibly
Storm could breathe easily underwater and looked
around herself with great curiosity. The others
experienced the same momentary panic, shock,
bewilderment and then relief that Maggie had, as
the merfolk breathed into them, enabling them to
become part of the ocean.

Further they swam, deeper and deeper, getting
closer to the sea bed and the city of Finfolkaheem.
Quinn reached out, testing his magical powers,
would they hold strong in the ocean? Vita too tested
her powers, she tentatively pulled at the currents in
the water, could she affect the tide? As he swam,
Archer reached into his ever present back pack
pulling out an armful of gadgets which he set to

adapting for underwater use. Storm grinned from ear to ear marvelling at the creatures all around them, she had never seen such unusual life forms and was completely mesmerised.

Although noise travels differently below water, all of them heard the warning sound at the same time. The alarm had been raised, they had been spotted! A huge merman astride an even more enormous seahorse galloped beneath them blowing through an enormous conch shell. The city loomed up on the sea bed in front of them and an army of finfolk spewed out, heading straight for the intruders.

Quinn motioned to James to take Storm so he could go and find Maggie whilst the others mounted an attack. Gathering all their courage, they swam strongly away from James, hoping the inevitable battle would give James enough cover to find and rescue Maggie and the rings. On land Quinn had given orders to cause no harm to any of the sea creatures if at all possible. The plan was to distract the finfolk for as long as it took to get Maggie out and then escape back to the island. Clearly the finfolk had other ideas; the front line of seahorses carried men and women who had fury in their eyes and sharp spears in their raised hands. At another signal from the conch shell, the spears were thrown in unison. The battle had begun.

Battle below the sea

Finn and his team of merfolk tried to lead the others into a defensive position behind some towering coral. No good. Whilst the first spears missed due to them shifting swiftly, the second attack hit the coral straight on, shattering it in all directions.

"Now", yelled Quinn, conjuring a protective shield. Vita pushed at the sea with all her might, palms facing out. A wave rippled away from her, building in strength and causing the third wave of spears to lose their speed and destabilised the front row of sea horses. Chaos erupted! The horses bucked and reared and a number of the merfolk lost their grip

on them.

Archer launched net after net, from a hand held canon, trapping and ensnaring several finfolk on their seahorses. Wave after wave of tidal attacks from Vita caused the finfolk to retreat; those that remained tumbled and fell into the nets. Each new spear they launched simply bounced off Quinn's shield. How long could they keep this up for though? Their strength could only last for so long and Archer's nets would dissolve before then. It was all down to James now. Lana, Galia, Finn and Jonas had vanished. Where were they? Had they changed their minds?

Meanwhile, James and Storm had snuck into Finfolkaheem, hiding amongst curtains of sea weed and thick waving kelp at every opportunity. James followed Storm, who had picked up her bond with Maggie, and they swam swiftly through the deserted city straight to the coral jail which was attached to an amazing, pearly palace. There was no time for James to appreciate the sheer artistry and skill

119

which had gone into carving and embellishing this architectural masterpiece; he was sure there would be guards at the jail entrance. But no! There wasn't a single guard, clearly all hands were required above to dispel the intruders. It really was a ghost town. Thanks to Storm it didn't take long to find Maggie but James quickly found that the lock on the cell door was complex and enchanted. Maggie hadn't sensed Storm approach, slumped as she was on a little bed at the back of the cell. She looked forlorn and dejected, worn out and discouraged. James rattled the cell door and Storm reached out with her senses, whimpering through the water. The sound travelled to Maggie, stirring her from her crest fallen state, and she slowly turned towards the door, raising her head in disbelief. She shook her head, as if she was dreaming and couldn't believe her eyes.

"James, Storm?", she murmured, "is that really you?"

"Yes! We need to get you out of here," James

12

confirmed, "are you OK, where are the rings, where do they keep the key for this lock?" The questions tumbled out of James as his eyes searched her hands for the rings. He could sense how dispirited she was and knew they had to get her out of there before she completely lost her confidence. Maggie shook her head.

She really wasn't OK, and she didn't know where the rings were hidden, and she had no idea where they kept the keys. James racked his brains, there had to be a solution. He sifted through the information stored in his mind, searching for all the potential places to keep treasure. A skeleton key was what they needed, a key which would open any door around the palace. Doubtless this key would be guarded heavily or kept on the Queen herself. What to do? Just then Storm growled, a sinister and eerie sound below the sea, and her hackles rose. Danger was imminent and Maggie pointed behind them, eyes aghast. It was Queen Merilla herself!

Escape

It all happened in a blur. Queen Merilla strode forward and cackled horribly to see James and Storm by Maggie's cell.

"What could be better?", she sneered, "a few more pets to play with. My guards will soon have the rest of your group too; interfering pests."

Then, quick as a flash, Storm leapt at the Queen's throat and tore off the chain holding the rings. There was no time for her to react. Storm shook her head to one side, flinging the chain towards the cell bars. Maggie caught it, grabbed the rings and pushed

123

them straight onto her fingers. The power surged through her instantly, banishing all her fears.

"Move!" she ordered James and Storm whilst raising her arms, palms facing out, and pushing the air towards the cell door. The doors blasted right off their hinges hitting Queen Merilla squarely in the chest. She shot back under its weight and crumpled to the floor.

"Is she dead?" James was shocked.

"Unconscious, let's move. The others need our help. Come on!" Maggie urged, taking the lead once more. They swam strongly out and away from the city, Maggie searching through Storm's memories to bring her up to speed. Moments later they came upon the battle action, arriving just in time, as the others were weakening under the sheer number of finfolk attacking them. Vita had used up her strength pushing and pulling the currents in the ocean and now was using the seaweed itself, twisting and twining it to capture the finfolk. Quinn was visibly shaking under the sheer effort of maintaining the

defence bubble around them and Archer was doing
a magnificent job of keeping up a steady attack. He
was now using The Sneaky, a favourite weapon of
his. He flung it out like a boomerang and it arced
gracefully around the finfolk, then back again. It
ejected streams of knock out gas which, although
slightly hampered being under water, caused several
of the seahorses to stumble, flail and plummet to the
sea bed below. Time was running out. Queen
Merilla would be awake in no time and would
doubtless join her soldiers. She had underestimated
Maggie and her friends once, but it wouldn't
happen twice.

Maggie used the ring's powers, which were
thrumming energy through every vein in her body,
to cause several things to happen at once. She let rip
a mighty wave, pushing the seahorses and guards
far back, giving her team time to gather their
reserves. She called out to the seahorses in her
mind, urging them to shake off their enslavement by
the finfolk and she called out to the sea creatures
she could sense all around her. Time to rally the

12

troops! Maggie was positively radiating energy and power as she joined the others. She reached out her hands resting them on each of her friends' shoulders in turn, boosting their dwindling reserves. There was no time for a lengthy reunion; already the finfolk were regrouping. They were without their seahorses who were in absolute chaos, shaking off their guards and careering around in a confused manner. Maggie had really spooked them and they didn't know which way to turn. Rows and rows of finfolk advanced, propelled by strong, muscular tails with their sharply pronged tridents held aloft. Suddenly the ocean behind Maggie's team churned and darkened and the eyes of the finfolk visibly widened. They started to slow their pace and retreated slightly. Maggie turned and her jaw dropped open at the sight.

A great pod of narwhals with their long, unicorn like horns, advanced ominously. Behind them came giant leopard seals, huge walruses, a pod of sinister orcas and last of all a giant blue whale. In amongst them swam sting rays, eels, needle fish, octopus,

sharks and millions of fish of every colour, size and shape. They moved as one gigantic shoal, neither pausing nor straying, locked on to their target; the finfolk. Finally, the seahorses rose up, joining their fellow creatures. The finfolk simply had no choice but to flee. Dropping tridents and scrambling to get past each other they retreated as fast as their tails could propel them. Maggie sent her thanks to the sea creatures and pointed upwards; it was time for them to complete their escape. Maggie drew the others up with her, and soon they were gasping fresh mouthfuls of air once more. Maggie wasn't finished though, she used the ocean's currents to carry them swiftly to shore and moments later they all strode on to the beach at Hether Blether. All but Maggie slumped to the sand, utterly exhausted. Maggie paced back and forth like a caged tiger, still buzzing with energy.

"Take them off!" called James. He was afraid she would burn up entirely. Maggie looked down at her hands and roughly pulled the rings off. The adrenalin instantly left her and she crashed down to her knees.

129

"Well, that's what you call team work!" Quinn tried to raise a smile. Finn, Jonas, Galia and Lana stared at the children in awe.

"I'm not quite sure what happened there." Finn murmured.

"Maggie happened. That's what." Quinn replied and this time the others started to giggle, then laugh and finally they all erupted into hysterics, the fear and drama of the battle pouring from them and being replaced with relief and elation. It was several moments before they fully subsided and Maggie slowly rose to her feet, waiting for the others to join her.

"Back home?" she queried looking Quinn directly in the eye. He nodded and readied himself to conjure the portal which would take them straight back to the Earthlie Realm. It was time to say goodbye to the merfolk on Hether Blether.

"You are now free to do as you please," Maggie

13

turned to them. 'Choose wisely." She turned away. They had helped in the end, but it would take a little while for her to shake of the feeling of entrapment caused by them.

Maggie reached out with her senses trying to reach Vince, Selene, Jedrek or any of the creatures back in their Realm, but they were too far away. Little did she know the anguish she would have picked up had she been able to reach them. With both rings missing from the Earthlie Realm things had taken a distinct turn for the worse.

CHAPTER 15

Home

"Any chance of a portal, Quinn?" , asked Maggie, "I think James and I need to check in at home too, it's been a while."

Quinn nodded. He had a much better idea of where they were in the world now and thought he could make it back to The Green. From there they could just head back through the Glimmer to the Earthlie Realm. It was harder than he thought though, with Hether Blether being so far from shore and with its own magical essence; it took every ounce of effort he had. The others watched as he furrowed his brow, muttered incantations and concentrated with all his might. Finally, after several agonising moments, a pale shimmering glimmer opened and they wasted no time in slipping through as quickly as they could. Maggie felt the now familiar whoosh as they travelled through the portal and she staggered out the other side, straight on to The Green. She felt disorientated and stumbled to her knees, panting heavily. After a few more minutes steadying herself, she smiled weakly in relief. It was all so normal. They exchanged hugs and made plans to meet up very soon. Maggie was just as anxious to see what was happening in The Earthlie Realm too. For now, she pushed the rings into Quinn's hands. Maggie wanted him to be the one to return them, as he had felt so terrible about banishing them with her. With a last wave, Maggie settled the trapdoor back down into its position and walked beside James towards their homes. They were both quietly mulling events over and Storm padded silently between them, looking from one to the other in turn, as if checking they were both really and truly safe.

"Hi mum," Maggie walked up to her mum who was

13

throwing a handful of corn into the hen run, "so glad to see you, love you." She wrapped her arms around her mum and squeezed her tightly, breathing in her familiar scent.

"Hello, hunny pie," her mum squeezed her tightly back, but raised one eyebrow, "did you have a good afternoon?" Maggie blinked a couple of times. Afternoon? Thank goodness her mum had no idea of all she had seen and done or she would never ever get over worrying about her and would probably ban her from leaving the house for ever.

"Is it tea time yet?" Storm interrupted her thoughts whilst also nuzzling Maggie's mum's legs.
"Just going to feed Storm and grab a snack." Maggie reluctantly let go of her mum, she didn't want to go worrying her by being all over the top with the hugging. Her mum had a sixth sense about that sort of thing and could somehow tell the difference between all sorts of hugs.

Storm devoured her tea in seconds as usual, licking

13

the bowl thoroughly to check there wasn't a single scrap left. Maggie was just wolfing down the last of a cheese and marmite sandwich, when all at once, there was a clamouring in her head. At the same time her mum called her back outside. Maggie glanced out of the window towards her mum who was talking to James and another boy. Was that Quinn? Meanwhile Vince, Selene, Jedrek and Imari were all vying for her attention in her mind. It was all coming through jumbled up and Storm was shaking her head to and fro, as if she was getting mixed messages too. Maggie quickened her step. The Earthlies were in trouble; that much was clear. Vince was repeatedly calling her, his voice sounding hoarse and panicky; none of his usual quips and jokes. Selene sounded rushed and serious too, and Imari joined in the chorus asking for her to come back immediately. What on earth was Quinn doing here and talking to her mum? It must be serious.

"Maggie love," said her mum, "James and his friend Quinn here have come to invite you out for tea if you would like? A picnic was it?"

"Yes," Quinn nodded, "over in the woods if that's
ok with you Mrs ….?" Quinn shimmered slightly
but luckily Maggie's mum didn't seem to notice.

"Call me Jo, Quinn. Well it's lovely to meet you and
nice to see you too James. If you'll excuse me I
must get back to my girls; just collecting their eggs.
You all enjoy yourselves, such a nice evening for a
picnic. Don't go too far and Maggie, 8 o'clock
latest. I want you home before dark."

Maggie gave her mum another quick hug for good
measure and raised both eyebrows at Quinn, not
daring to speak until they got out of earshot.
"What are you doing here?" she hissed as soon as
they got out of her gate, "what's going on, Vince is
going crazy, and the others, I can hear everyone,
what's happening?"
"Chaos, Maggie, for days. We couldn't wait any
longer, I had to come and get you."
"Days? What do you mean? I just finished my
sandwich! You gave the rings back right?
"Of course, to Keithia, right away. She's really

13

relieved about that, but while we were away the whole place went crazy! There have been all sorts of attacks from different Realms. It's going to take a while for things to settle down. Meanwhile Keithia needs your help with something."

"What? Where? You're kidding right? We just got back! James, did you know about this?"
James shook his head looking puzzled and anxious again. Storm was complaining loudly in Maggie's head and Maggie was trying desperately to block out her mutterings.

"Here we go again, I mean honestly, can't a puppy get some rest? I really think it is nap time. I am really, really missing my comfy bed you know? Not even a quick snooze or anything!" But the loyal pup kept close to Maggie; for all her grumbling there was no way she was going to let Maggie out of her sight for a second, especially considering what had happened the last time she did. She had only just got her back!

Quinn pulled up the trapdoor and ushered them all through the Glimmer.

"Keithia will explain everything and we need James to get some extra background. Also, how are you with heights?"

Maggie grinned at James' horrified face, she knew he definitely did not like heights whatsoever, but as for her, "Love them, the higher the better! You should know me by now Quinn, lead the way!"

Book 5 - Victory in the Sky Realm

The adventure continues from where it left off in Book 4.

An adventurous and magical quest for daring readers.

Are you ready to join the team for the ultimate challenge? Will they be able to face up to the evil Queen, The deadly Morrigan? Will this last adventure in the first series of Below The Green, be the final challenge of all?

The team travel far and wide through new portals to track down crucial clues and ultimately must enter a terrifying new Realm; The Sky Realm. They have never seen anything like it and must work together like never before. Using new skills and weapons they attempt to pull off a dangerous rescue, solve an ancient curse and bring harmony to the Earthlie Realm once and for all. But, as usual, things are never quite what they seem and

141

this dark force is unbelievably powerful. Who will return and what will be sacrificed for the cause? Get ready for an edge of your seat, gripping, roller coaster of a read. An epic finale awaits!

Keep reading for a teaser about book 5...

CHAPTER 1

Back in the Earthlie Realm

"Butterflies?" queried Maggie, "what do you mean a cloud of butterflies?"

"You'll see", responded Quinn to Maggie and James, as all three children and Storm hurtled down the steps from the trapdoor heading straight for the clearing. "I've never seen anything like it before, they seem to have come over from the Isle of Integrity, in the Lake of Furies."

Maggie shot him a curious glance, she had never heard mention of such places before but she held her breath for the journey and within a few

143

impatient moments they skidded to a halt before a gathering in the clearing. Keithia was amongst them looking uncharacteristically anxious.

"Come Maggie," Keithia, The Ancient from the School of Nature and Nurture, began, "there is no time to lose. We have been under heavy attack for weeks but, thanks to you all for returning the Alpha and Omega Rings, we are starting to push back our enemies and some small measure of restoration has begun. There is much to do however. Also, a grave misfortune has befallen the Realm and we need your skills to assist us."

"Anything," replied Maggie instantly, "however I can help I will."

"The thing is, we are not entirely sure what has happened yet, but what we do know is that the Druidess Aine, from the Isle of Integrity, has sent a group of her messengers to summon us. This has never happened in my life time and I need you to hear what the messengers have to say."

"The butterflies?" Maggie queried.

"Yes, follow me. They have swarmed by the shoreline of The Lake of Furies. Quinn, if you will, please? James, Madeleine and Melville await you." Keithia nodded at each in turn and looked expectantly at Quinn.

Quinn cut the air with one hand whilst muttering an incantation. A portal instantly glimmered before them. Very efficient, Maggie mused, her friend had really come a long way from their first journey to the Realm of the Grimms. It honestly seemed that first adventure had taken place a lifetime ago though in reality less than a year had gone by.

Keithia, Maggie and Storm stepped through the portal ahead of Quinn who neatly zipped the Glimmer shut with another deft hand movement.

Maggie gasped at the breathtaking view ahead. Which was more spectacular? The magnificent lake, which in truth looked more like an ocean?

145

The shoreline was wider than she could detect and the water reached further than she could see. It glistened and glinted, edged with lush, beautiful foliage. Or the cloud of butterflies? That was something else again! Maggie had seen a murmuration of starlings before in Upland, which was always a wonder of nature at dawn and dusk, but the view before ahead was even more incredible than that! An airy, luminous, billowing cloud of shimmering white butterflies bloomed and swayed like seaweed. It was utterly mesmerising and the unearthly sounds of thousands, perhaps tens of thousands, of whirring butterfly wings filled the air around them. Maggie was drawn instinctively towards them and they turned, as one, as if sensing her arrival. Like a heavenly blessing, they drifted down towards her, settling on and around her; until she could no longer be seen. Quinn, Keithia and Storm kept their distance and Keithia indicated with her hands that they should allow Maggie to go forward alone. Storm whimpered a little, but she could sense that Maggie was safe and calm. Several minutes passed, and then, just as lightly, the cloud

14

lifted, turned, and fanned out like a long swarm of honey bees, back over the lake until it could no longer be seen at all. Maggie walked back towards the others with a contemplative look on her face.

"I have been summoned by the Druidess Aine to come to the Isle of Integrity. No one else may join me on the journey but she promised me safe passage, whether we choose to undertake her Quest or not. She has heard that I have joined the School of Noble Beasts; the butterflies tell her everything it seems. I have already agreed to go and meet her. They have gone to inform her, and she will send another messenger to fetch me; her daughter, the Druidess Niamh. Once I have gone, please ask James to find out all the information he has on the Island and it's inhabitants. Plus, I think I'm going to need the whole team this time; Vince, Imari and Selene too. Please could you bring Britta and Wolfe to meet me here on my return. I'm not sure how long I will be, I don't think more than a day, but I will need to ask for their advice before we set off."

No sooner had Maggie finished speaking than the sound of water bubbling and rushing met their ears. The lake began to churn and froth at the edges, and in the distance another luminous speck appeared. It wasn't the same as the butterflies though. This didn't seem gentle and calm, and they all stepped back a few paces whilst peering into the distance, to see whether it was friend or foe.

"I think it's Niamh," Maggie whispered half to herself, "she rides a white horse which can travel over water, the butterflies told me."

Sure enough, as their eyes adjusted and the creature drew closer, they could detect a huge, magnificent, regal white horse thundering toward them. It sent wave upon wave of much smaller white horses crashing onto the shores and spraying them completely with fresh cool water.

Silence followed this dramatic arrival of the Druidess, who smiled benignly at them, whilst reaching down a hand to help Maggie jump up

14

behind her. It was a matter of seconds before the stately creature turned on it's lofty hooves and with an impressive buck, and rearing impossibly high, it galloped back across the lake, soon disappearing into the distant mists leaving silence in their wake.

Quinn and Keithia exchanged glances, whilst Storm whimpered in earnest. She did not like this at all, not one bit. It hurt her deeply to be separated from Maggie and she just knew there was bound to be danger ahead. Quinn and Keithia knew it too, they could all feel it in their bones, but none could have had the slightest inkling of what really lay ahead.

They were all now on an inescapable path, ending in a decisive battle with the ultimate Queen of Fury. A great and venomous Queen, the evil Druidess of battle and death was none other than The Morrigan.

Shanty Realm Bonfire Treat Recipe

The Finfolk enjoy a special treat cooked in the bonfire as the embers die down late at night. See below for the recipe for this delicious baked banana treat!

Ingredients:

One banana per person.

A couple of marshmallows per banana.

Some chunks of chocolate – the Finfolk like sea salted caramel chunks too.

Tinfoil to wrap them in.

Method:

1. Keep the banana in its skin, but cut length ways through it almost all the way through.

2. Push the chocolate, marshmallows and any other treats inside and then wrap up in tinfoil.

3. Nestle the banana into glowing embers as the fire dies down. Leave for several minutes to let it bake.

4. Use tongs to take them out and scoop out the delicious mixture, serve with cream or ice cream if you like!

Enjoy!

Dear Reader,

Thank you for reading book 4 which I hope you enjoyed as much as I loved writing it. The tension is really rising for the last in the first series, book 5, Victory in the Sky Realm. I know you are going to be ready to join the team in this epic challenge. It is packed full of twists and turns and will keep you on the edge of your seat. You will not be able to put this next book down! For those of you who have asked me for a new Realm, then let me know what you think! I created this once especially for you. If you haven't been in touch yet, then I would love to hear which is your favourite Realm and character and where you would like to see the team travel to next. I will let you in on a secret…I am already researching new challenges and Realms for series two! Think polar bears, hot African sun, evil villains and all sorts of new quests, magical skills, weapons and some adorable new characters. See you in book 5, Victory in The Sky Realm.

Best wishes

AR Hetherington

15

Printed in Great Britain
by Amazon